Steven,

Holiday Holdup

Steven,

Real heroes read!

This book is fiction. The people, places, events, and crooked candy bandits depicted within are fictitious. Any resemblance to persons living or dead or to real life places is purely coincidence and, in all honesty, probably a little disturbing.

ISBN 978-0-9785642-5-4

Printed in the U.S.A.

First Printing, June 2009

You Better Watch Out, You Better Not Fight ...
You Better Not Doubt I'm Stealing This Night ...

Candy Claws Is Coming To Town!

CONTENTS

Real Heroes Read!
realheroesread.com

#8: Holiday Holdup

David Anthony
and
Charles David

Illustrations
Lys Blakeslee

Traverse City, MI

Home of the Heroes

abigail

andrew

zoë

CHAPTER 1:
MEET THE HEROES

Welcome to Traverse City, Michigan, population 18,000. The city has everything you might expect: malls, movie theaters, schools, and playgrounds. Kids swim here in the summer and build snowmen during the winter. Sometimes they pretend that they live in an ordinary place.

But Traverse City is far from ordinary. It is set on one of the Great Lakes and attracts tourists in every season. Thousands of people visit every year.

Still, few of them know the city's real secret. Even fewer talk about it. You see, Traverse City is home to three hardy superheroes. This story is about them.

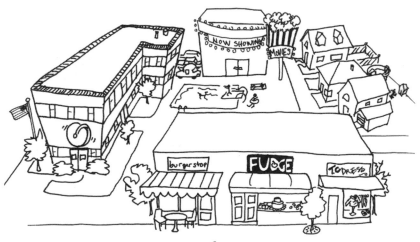

Meet Abigail, the oldest of our heroes by a whole eight minutes. When it comes to sports, she can't be beat—not at hurdles, not at hitting homeruns, and certainly not at hockey. Every year when the family picks out a Christmas tree, she can single-handedly deliver it safely onto the roof of the car. Too bad the tree toss isn't an event in the Winter Olympics.

Andrew comes next. He's Abigail's twin brother, younger by a measly eight minutes. If it has wheels, Andrew can ride it. From Hum-vees to Harleys, he's hip, happening, and a hotdog on wheels. On Christmas Eve, it's his job to wrap the tree in lights.

Round and round, there he goes.
When he stops, everything glows.

Last but definitely not least is Baby Zoë. She's
proof that big things can come in small packages.
She still wears a diaper, but only she can put the star
on top of the Christmas tree without a stepladder.
She puts the *her* in *hero*.

Together these three heroes keep the streets and neighborhoods of Traverse City, Michigan, and America safe. Together they are …

CHAPTER 2:
HO-HO-HORRIFIED

"*H-h*-horrified," Zoë whimpered, hiding behind her sister.

It was Christmas Eve afternoon, and she and her siblings were at the Grand Traverse Mall. Colorful lights sparkled in every window. Holiday carols played from every store.

Zoë should have felt happy and safe, but she was terrified. Why?

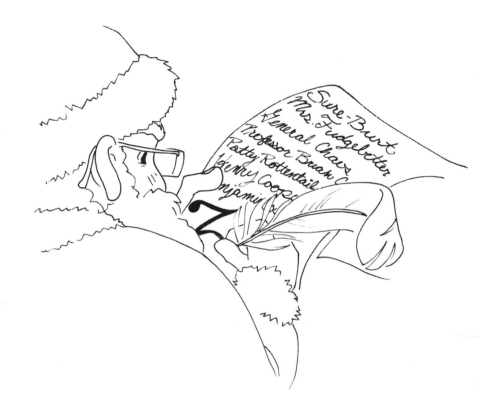

Because she was waiting in line to see Santa Claus. Almost nothing frightened her more.

Think about it. The pressure, the stress. One slip in Santa's presence and she would be put on the Naughty List. That would mean no presents on Christmas morning and coal in her stocking.

Abigail smiled at her little sister. Poor Zoë! She remembered being afraid to sit on Santa's lap years ago. Mom and Dad had even taken a picture of it once. Now they kept the photograph above the fireplace for everyone to see. Humiliating!

So she tried to cheer Zoë up. One family photograph of a sobbing superhero was enough.

Out of her duffel bag Abigail pulled three balls. First she placed a basketball on the tip of her index finger and spun it. Nice trick but nothing new. Zoë had seen that before and wasn't impressed.

So Abigail made it more challenging. She added two more balls to her act. Tada! Instant indoor snowman.

"I call this trick the Triple Frosty." She grinned proudly.

Abigail's trick worked on Zoë, but it didn't impress their brother. Andrew didn't even look their way.

He had bigger things on his mind. *Longer* things. Like his Christmas list. It was huge. Andrew had been working on it for weeks now. Name something with wheels—anything—and it was probably on the list. Twice.

Andrew didn't want Santa to miss anything. Pretty thoughtful of him, don't you think?

Finally the line moved, and it was the heroes' turn to see Santa. Abigail and Andrew sprang forward eagerly, but they had to drag Zoë.

"Come on, Zoë," Andrew pleaded.

"It'll be fun," Abigail promised. "Trust us."

Zoë didn't believe them. They were talking about Santa. Kris to the Kringle. He was sitting so close he could hear them!

Her eyes widened, and her knees started to shake.

"Help!" she squealed, trying to fly away.

Luckily Zoë didn't get far. The twins snatched her ankles before she could escape. Then they shoved her roughly onto Santa's lap. So much for peace on Earth.

"Ho-ho-ho!" chuckled Santa. Predictable, maybe, but comforting, too.

Zoë relaxed immediately and took a deep breath. She wanted to be sure Santa heard what she wanted for Christmas.

"Hippo!" she shouted at the top of her lungs. She wanted a hippopotamus, just like the singer in her favorite Christmas song.

The cracking sound that followed was that of Santa's glasses breaking. He had heard her, all right. So had everyone else in the Grand Traverse Mall.

CHAPTER 3:
CANDY BANDITS

Later that night, Zoë's parents tucked her into bed. They each kissed a cheek and told her to sleep tight. Sugarplums and all that.

When they left, Zoë tried to sleep tight. She really did. She squeezed her eyes shut. She tossed and turned. She even counted reindeer.

Sure, most people counted sheep, but it was Christmastime. Reindeer were much more appropriate. She knew that Santa would agree.

When she did eventually fall asleep, it wasn't for long. Even her imaginary reindeer had fallen asleep before her.

A noise woke her after midnight. *Clippity-clop. Cloppity-clip.*

Zoë sat straight up. "Huh?" she muttered, rubbing the sleep from her eyes.

The noise came again. *Clippity-clop. Cloppity-clip.* Could it be Dancer and Prancer tap-dancing on the roof?

Zoë bolted for the window and threw open the curtain. Would she spot reindeer? Santa's sleigh? The Big Man in Red himself?

She held her breath and peered into the night. A light snow was falling. Christmas lights glowed from nearby windows. Sleighs and dozens of reindeer filled the sky.

Zoë blinked in surprise. Sleighs? Dozens of reindeer? Santa was supposed to have just one sleigh pulled by nine reindeer. What was going on here?

Suddenly Andrew and Abigail threw open Zoë's door.

"Santa's here!" they exclaimed together.

"We heard him on the roof," Abigail explained without taking a breath. "Let's sneak downstairs and watch."

"Maybe he's eating the cookies we baked," Andrew added.

Zoë just nodded. Obviously her brother and sister hadn't looked outside. They wouldn't be talking about cookies if they had. But there wasn't time to explain. The twins were already heading for the stairs.

So Zoë joined them, and the three heroes tiptoed downstairs. Like secret spies they silently peeked around the corner.

"Horrors!" Zoë gasped at what she and her siblings saw in the family room. It was like a scene out of The Grinch, only worse because it was really happening.

Five strange creatures had broken into their home. They were as tall as Santa's elves but not nearly as friendly. They were bandits—candy bandits—not toy makers. They looked like giant candy canes with eyes and arms, and wore pointed green caps and thin black masks.

The heroes froze at the sight of them. The candy bandits laughed. The bandits were stealing presents from under the tree. Christmas was going to be ruined!

26

CHAPTER 4:
HOLIDAY HOLDUP

Dressed in bathrobes and slippers, Mom and Dad burst out of their room. They charged down the stairs, into the family room, and stood protectively in from of the heroes.

"Stay back, kids," Dad said in his deepest voice.

"We're being robbed!" Mom added.

Two bandits spotted them and dropped a large present. They pulled candy cane rifles out of their nearby loot sack and took aim at Mom and Dad.

"This is a holdup," the first bandit sneered. "Yeah," agreed the second. "A holiday holdup."

"How dare you!" Dad exclaimed. He snatched an umbrella from a hook near the front door and dashed into the family room. "Get out of our house. It's Christmas Eve!"

The two bandits watched him calmly. As he closed in on them, they squeezed the triggers on their candy cane rifles and fired.

Z-z-z-zap!

Icy beams like frozen lasers burst from the rifles. One struck Dad high. One struck him low. Both froze him to the floor and covered him in snow.

Dad had been turned into a human snowman!

Mom yelped and sprinted after Dad. She ran almost as quickly as sporty Abigail. Who knew? Maybe Mom had superpowers of her own.

"You're not Santa's little helpers!" she shrieked at the bandits. "You're nothing but candy-coated criminals!"

This time when the "elves" fired their rifles, they also cackled like bullies packing icy snowballs. They were enjoying themselves. *Z-z-z-zap!*

In seconds Mom was a snowman, too.

The candy bandits didn't wait to fire again. They shifted their aim from Mom directly to the stairway.

"Look out!" Andrew howled, pushing his sisters up the steps.

Z-z-z-zap!

But he needn't have bothered. The bandits weren't shooting at him or at his sisters. They were firing at the opening at the bottom of the stairway.

They were filling it with ice. Building a wall. And the heroes were trapped on the other side.

CHAPTER 5:
ABIGAIL AVALANCHE

Andrew and Zoë pounded on the wall of ice with their fists. *Brrr* and ouch! The wall was freezing cold and at least two feet thick. Breaking it would take more than punches and bare skin.

"Give me some room please," Abigail requested. Unlike her siblings, she had already realized that fists wouldn't break the ice. She was perched at the top of the stairs, wearing downhill snow skis and a crash helmet.

"What are you going to do?" Andrew smirked up the stairs at his twin. "The Staircase Slalom?"

"Hair-brained," Zoë snickered, nudging her brother in the ribs.

Abigail responded by planting her poles and leaning forward. "More like the Abigail Avalanche," she said. "Now watch out!"

Then she cranked her shoulders and bent her knees. *Voom!* She started cruising down the stairs on her skis. Andrew and Zoë barely managed to leap out of her way in time.

At the last moment, Abigail turned sharply and lowered her head. She was a human battering ram. Next stop, family room.

CRASH!

She hit the icy wall headfirst and plowed through it like a wrecking ball. Good thing she was wearing a helmet!

Blocks of ice, shards, and splinters burst into the family room. So did Abigail. Her arms, legs, skis, and poles went flying every which way.

"Hurry!" Zoë cried, pointing at the fireplace.

Standing inside it was the last bandit in the room. The others had vanished, probably up the chimney. The remaining bandit was trying to follow them, but it was also pushing a bulky bag up the chimney.

"There go our presents!" Abigail exclaimed.

Then *pop!* the bag disappeared up the chimney.

The bandit gave the heroes one last sneer. "Don't look so sour," he teased. "Here, have some candy."

He tossed a handful of sugary treats at the heroes, and then scrambled up the chimney. The bandit and their Christmas presents were gone.

CHAPTER 6:
NORTH POLE BLACK HOLE

"Follow that bandit!" Abigail cried, sprinting toward the fireplace. She and her siblings had climbed the chimney before. They could do it again.

Zoë and Andrew didn't budge. They were staring out the front window. Their house wasn't the only one being robbed. Every house on their street was swarming with candy bandits.

"It isn't just our house," Andrew said quietly. "Those bandits are everywhere. They're stealing Christmas!"

"Hundreds," Zoë confirmed.

Abigail froze, one hand on the fireplace mantle. "Do you think something happened to Santa?" she asked. "Maybe someone should check on him."

By someone, Abigail meant Zoë. Her baby sister could fly and had actually been to the North Pole before.* Zoë wouldn't need a map or directions to get there again.

"Hasta la vista," Zoë shouted, zipping up the chimney. Goodbye!

Apparently she didn't need to be asked twice either. Santa could be in danger!

*See Heroes A2Z #1: Alien Ice Cream

At first Zoë flew northward with confidence and determination. She would find Santa, she promised herself. Find him and then stop those nasty candy bandits that were stealing Christmas.

But the trip to the North Pole was long and cold. It gave Zoë time to think, and that gave her time to worry.

She had never been up so late before. Certainly not outside and alone and flying in the dark. How she wished Rudolph were there to keep her company!

When she finally reached the North Pole, Zoë almost missed Santa's castle. Everything was black. There were no lamps, no Christmas lights, no reindeer with shiny noses.

Santa's castle looked like a ghost town!

"*H*-hello?" Zoë called, but all that answered her was the wind. She was alone.

Santa, his elves, and his reindeer were gone. Christmas would have to be cancelled!

CHAPTER 7:
SNEAKING ON THE SLEIGH

Zoë flew home from the North Pole in half the time it took her to get there. She wasn't just a little worried now. She was a lot confused.

Santa had disappeared. So had his elves and reindeer. It was as if they had all decided to skip Christmas this year. Maybe take a Hawaiian vacation.

Zoë could imagine but not believe.

Nor could she believe what had happened at home while she'd been gone. Traverse City was lost! Snowmen filled the streets. Reindeer with candy cane antlers tramped on every roof. Candy bandits shot and snowed anything that moved. It was like a game of freeze tag without end. No time-outs here.

Zoë found her siblings in the backyard. They were pressed up against the tool shed, spying on the bandits.

"How?" Zoë asked, dismayed by how bad the trouble had gotten.

Abigail and Andrew didn't answer. They were too busy discussing a daring, dangerous plan to rescue Christmas.

They decided to follow the candy bandits by sneaking onto a sleigh. If Christmas was going to be stolen, the heroes were going to go with it. No one messed with Santa Claus on their watch.

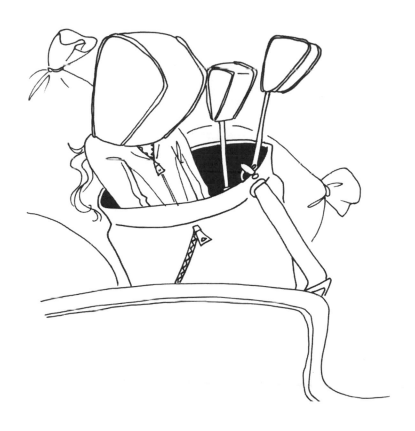

"Here I go," Abigail whispered, taking off at a run through the snow.

In an amazing display of athletics, she bolted across the backyard, high-jumped onto the house, and sprang into the sleigh. One, two, three—perfect score. She landed in a golf bag on the sleigh and did her best to look like just another club.

"I wonder if this present is for me?" she thought out loud.

Andrew followed closely behind her, amazing in his own way. He didn't run or jump. Those were his sister's specialties. He borrowed a spare snow tire from the tool shed and rolled across the backyard, up the side of the house, and onto the roof. Don't try that with just any old tire!

Then he scrambled under the sleigh and grabbed onto the runners. If the sleigh had wheels, that was where they would be. Hiding there made sense to Andrew.

Zoë hid last but not least. She took a choice spot at the top of an open Santa-like toy sack. With a ribbon in her hair, she looked like the perfect baby doll.

Introducing Cuddle-Me-Zoë. She cries, she flies, she packs a big surprise. Hug her and she says, "Hugs!" But don't let her hug you, because she doesn't know here own strength.

After hiding, the heroes didn't wait long before the sleigh moved. A bandit took the reins, snapped them, and shouted:

On Pirate, on Plunder, on Thunder and Lightning!
On Swindle, on Smuggle, on Poacher and Frightening!

The reindeer leaped into a gallop and then bounded off the roof. Giddyup! They were flying, and so were the heroes.

But where were they flying to?

CHAPTER 8:
SOUTH FOR THE WINTER

"South," Andrew said to himself. The reindeer and sleigh were traveling south. Away from Traverse City and definitely not toward the North Pole.

Still, south could lead to so many places. To Lansing, Michigan's capital. To the Huckleberry Railroad in Flint, a great place to visit during the holidays. Even beyond Michigan to a city like Cleveland, Ohio, where the heroes had saved the world from Benjamin Axe and his Heavy Metal Hydra.*

*See Heroes A2Z #7: Guitar Rocket Star

Andrew tried to concentrate on the sights below, but it wasn't easy in the dark. He thought he saw lakes and rivers, roads, and forests on the tops of mountains.

"Where are we going?" he wondered. By now, Michigan was far, far away.

He knew that for certain when the bright lights of a giant amusement park shone below like a colorful ocean. In their glow, he spotted rides, hotels, and crazy buildings of all shapes and sizes.

The sleigh had flown farther south than he had realized. It was crossing over the Magic Kingdom in Orlando, Florida.

The sleigh had traveled hundreds of miles in just minutes. No wonder Santa could normally cover so much territory in one night.

Speaking of Santa, a call came in for the sleigh's driver.

"Come in, Sweettooth," a big voice boomed on the phone. "This is Mr. Claus. Report at once."

The candy bandit driver scrambled to answer his phone immediately. Naturally it looked like a candy cane.

Mr. Claus? The heroes couldn't believe their ears. Santa was calling one of the bandits that had stolen Christmas. It sounded as if the two of them were working together.

"Report," the voice repeated. "Where are you?"

The bandit stuttered in response. "Off the c-coast of *Ch*-Chile. Not much *f*-farther."

Chile, not chilly, as in the country on the southern tip of South America. So why, then, was the bandit stuttering? Not because of the temperature. Maybe it was afraid of a Santa Claus who would steal Christmas.

"Hurry it up," Mr. Claus snarled, ending the conversation.

Click. The phone went dead, and the bandit shivered. Again it had nothing to do with the temperature. It was cold outside, yes, but Santa was behaving colder.

So cold, in fact, that the heroes weren't too surprised by what they saw next. It made sense in a chilling sort of way.

The South Pole came into view. Nowhere was colder. Upon it sat the world's largest snow globe. How large? Large enough to hold an entire city inside it.

"Spike it," Abigail hissed, meaning it was time to stop, huddle up, and think of a new plan. Quarterbacks called the spike play in desperate situations.

And this situation was desperate.

The giant snow globe changed everything. It reminded Abigail of the Death Star from Star Wars, and the sleigh was heading straight for it.

"Hop?" Zoë suggested. She wanted to jump.

Abigail nodded and counted fast. "One, two, three!" Then she and her siblings leaped from the sleigh and started falling to the sharp, jagged ice below.

CHAPTER 9:
INFLATABLE SKATABLES

One great thing about being a superhero, Zoë could fly. One bad thing? Her brother and sister couldn't. So when the pair fell, they had to think fast or be flat, and not in a musical way.

"Helpless!" Zoë wailed, watching them plummet. She could probably catch one of her siblings in time. Save one and let the other fall. But which one—Abigail or Andrew? That wasn't a choice she wanted to make.

Thankfully a little Christmas magic came to the rescue, and Zoë didn't need to choose. Last holiday, Andrew had received the perfect gift for just such an emergency: inflatable skatables. What were those? Tennis shoes with inflatable wheels built right into their soles.

"There's no place like home!" Andrew shouted, sounding like Dorothy in The Wizard of Oz. Then he clicked his heels together and the inflatable skatables' wheels popped out. *Sproing!* He and his sister landed safely on the ice. Once—*boing*—twice—*boing*—thrice!

Safe on the ground, the heroes gazed at the giant snow globe in awe. There really was a whole city in there. A sparkling white city straight out of the pages of a Christmas fairy tale.

"It's beautiful," Abigail whispered.

"Hypnotizing," said Zoë.

They stared with their mouths open, and Andrew wanted to pinch them. In fact, he did just that. Honk, honk!

"Hey!" his sisters exclaimed together.

"Hey what?" Andrew fired back.

"Hey, quit goofing around," Abigail said.

"Hey, good idea."

"Hey, what do horses eat?"

"Oats," Andrew answered. "Or did you expect me to say 'hay?'"

Zoë cut them off. "Here," she said, pointing. She had spotted a back door that led into the giant snow globe.

Sounded simple enough. Too bad it was guarded by two penguins sitting on polar bears like medieval knights on horses.

CHAPTER 10:
HUNGRY HOMEWORK

Penguins on polar bears? Crazy! It sounded like the name of a Dr. Seuss book. One bear, two bear. Bite bear, chew bear. A book no one would dare to read.

"I don't think they're going to invite us inside," Abigail said.

"Unless it's for dinner," Andrew added.

The heroes were hiding behind a mound of snow, spying on the guards outside the giant snow globe. The penguins didn't worry them much, but the polar bears looked hungry.

Come to think of it, all polar bears looked hungry.

"Hoodwink," Zoë said, changing the subject. She didn't want to think about hungry polar bears, but they had given her an idea.

She and her siblings could trick the guards. Hoodwink them. They could out-scare the scary bears.

Andrew got right to it. Using his superpowers, he rolled three very large snow boulders. They were too big to throw but not quite large enough to flatten a house. In other words, perfect for scaring.

Zoë stacked the boulders. Only she could lift them and fly them to the top. Then she floated back and watched her sister dig through her duffel bag.

Abigail added the final touches. Hockey pucks for eyes, and more for buttons. Football for a nose. Downhill skis and baseball mitts for arms and hands. A jump rope for a mouth.

Tada, giant snowman. Or, the heroes hoped, giant snow monster.

When the snow monster was ready, Zoë and Andrew pushed it forward. Abigail waved its arms threateningly. *Rawr!*

The penguin guards crossed their candy cane spears as the heroes approached. They had the door completely blocked.

"Who goes there?" they demanded.

Abigail glanced down at her siblings. What should I say? she asked silently.

Zoë answered for her in a fake deep voice.

"Homework," she growled at the penguins. According to her brother and sister, nothing was worse than homework. Knowing that, it was the scariest name she could think of.

The penguins fidgeted nervously. They hadn't ever expected to see a giant talking snowman monster named Homework.

One of them cleared its throat, trying to sound brave. "*W*-what do you want?" it asked in a croak.

Ha! The heroes' hoodwink was working. The penguins were scared. Zoë decided to give them something to really worry about.

"Hungry!" she roared, and Abigail shook the snow monster's arms.

The penguins and polar bears fled. So much for trying to sound brave. Homework the hungry snow monster was too terrifying.

"Happy Holidays!" Zoë called after them. She figured they were already scared and on the run. No need to rub it in by frightening them more.

The penguins pulled up rein, stopped, and turned around. "Happy what?" they demanded suspiciously. Then one of them noticed Zoë.

"That's not a monster!" it squawked. "That's a baby in a diaper. Get it!"

So close! The heroes' plan had almost worked. Homework the hungry snow monster had nearly frightened away the penguins and polar bears.

Now, however, they were twice as determined to do their job. Keep trespassers out. That meant keeping the heroes out. No one fooled a penguin and got away with it!

The heroes turned to run, but the ice under their feet made it almost impossible to move. They would never have time to escape.

CHAPTER 11:
SKATE AN EIGHT

"I'm stuck!" Andrew cried, spinning his wheels. For real, too. He meant it. He had changed into his superhero costume and become Kid Roll. That was like Peter Parker turning into Spider-man. Same person, two identities.

The problem with his superhero identity now was that Kid Roll wasn't wearing snow tires. He needed chains or spikes to roll across the ice.

Zoë wasn't having any better luck. Ice and snow had frozen her cape, and flying that way was dangerous. It messed up her steering. So she was forced to try to run on the ice in her socks. She didn't get any farther than Andrew.

Andrew and Zoë were getting nowhere. Or should we say *snow*-where? The South Pole was too slippery for them to get going.

That meant Abigail had to come to the rescue. She had changed, too, and was now dressed as Triple-A, the All-American Athlete. Usually she wore running shoes or cleats. Today she wore Bauer hockey skates, just like the pros!

"Hurry!" Zoë shouted at Abigail, who could drag her and Andrew to safety. The penguins and polar bears were closing in.

But Abigail didn't come for her siblings. She winked at them, spun in a 180, and then started skating hard toward the penguins.

"Look out!" Andrew cried, about as useful as his wheels on ice.

Swisssh! Abigail cut hard to her right. *Swisssh!* Then to her left. Back and forth she skated, going round and round in a familiar pattern.

The penguins stopped again, confused. Abigail was skating circles around them. Why?

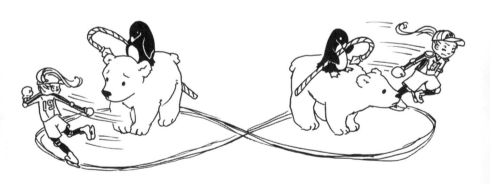

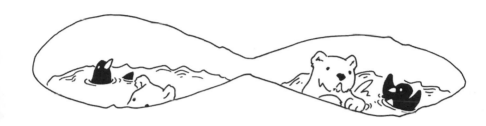

Splash! That's why.

Abigail hadn't skated in just random circles. She had skated in two very precise circles. Two *connected* circles.

She had skated in a figure eight.

And the penguins were in the middle of it.

So when Abigail's skates sliced through the ice, the penguins went two places. First they went down. Then they went into the water.

Double *splash!* Goodbye.

Polar bears and penguins could swim, so the heroes didn't stick around. They scampered, scrambled, and scuttled over the ice to the door in the giant snow globe.

"Are you ready for this?" Andrew asked, his hand on the doorknob.

Abigail narrowed her eyes. "Are you?" she asked. "Quit stalling or we'll think you're chicken."

"Ha!" Zoë chuckled, amused. Good one, Abigail.

Andrew frowned and threw open the door. Stalling? Not a chance. He would show them.

But the truth was, he wasn't ready. Neither were his sisters. The giant snow globe was like nothing they had seen before.

CHAPTER 12:
SUGARGLOBE CITY

"Sweet," Andrew said when he and his sisters entered the giant snow globe. He meant wow, cool, awesome. But he could have meant yum.

An arched sign greeted the heroes. In red-and-white-striped lettering it read, "Welcome to Sugarglobe City." Not *Snow*globe City.

Zoë stuck out her tongue and caught several snowflakes that were falling. A smile brightened her face.

"Heavenly," she said, licking her lips.

Abigail and Andrew quickly caught some flakes, too.

"It's sweet, all right!" Abigail exclaimed. "The snowflakes are made of sugar!"

No wonder the place was named Sugarglobe City. Sugar fell from the sky like snowflakes. Delicious!

Without paying attention to where he was going, Andrew wandered forward with his tongue out. His eyes were on the sky.

Bonk! He promptly ran into the side of a building and got a mouthful of brick. He crinkled his nose and smacked his lips. Make that cube, not brick. As in sugar cube. The whole building was made of sugar, too!

Everything in Sugarglobe City was made of sugar. The snow, the signs, the streetlights, and the stores. All of them sugar. The same went for mailboxes, malls, wagons, and windows. Sweet, sticky sugar.

"We could eat everything here," Abigail observed.

Her siblings were already trying to do just that. Zoë had flown to the top of a streetlight and was licking it like a lollypop. Andrew was chewing on its base like an old dog gnawing on a shoe.

"Stop it, you two!" Abigail scolded her siblings. "This is serious. Christmas has been stolen, remember?"

Zoë and Andrew wiped their mouths and stood up straight. There was nothing like getting caught with your hand in the cookie jar. Or in this case, your tongue on the streetlight.

"Look," Abigail continued, pointing overhead. "There go more sleighs."

As the heroes watched, sleigh after sleigh whisked past above. All of them were flying in the same direction. All of them were packed and piled high with presents.

"They're heading for that building," Andrew said, also pointing.

At the far end of the street stood a long, flat building. A sign in block letters named it *Presents Are the Past*. The sleighs were landing on it like F-16s on an aircraft carrier.

Sneaking carefully as if approaching the enemy base in a game of capture-the-flag, the heroes dashed toward the building. They crouched low to the ground and darted from doorway to doorway down the street.

Getting inside was simple. Huge garage doors stood open, displaying stolen Christmas presents for everyone to see.

What a sight! Stacks of brightly wrapped gifts reached the ceiling like the treasure in a dragon's hoard. Merry Christmas and goodnight!

A candy bandit carrying a clipboard walked into view.

"Michigan, U.S.A. is finished, sir," it said. "Soon North America will be yours."

"Good," said a familiar low voice.

Santa! How dare he! The heroes nearly gave away their hiding spot and rushed forward.

But when the speaker appeared, the heroes froze. He wasn't Santa Claus. He wasn't anyone they had seen before. He was round and red, but not jolly or an elf. He wore a striped outfit and had long, curved fingernails like candy canes.

He was also, without a doubt, the one who had stolen Christmas.

CHAPTER 13:
CLAUS VS. CLAWS

"Hostage!" Zoë gasped. Suddenly everything became clear to her. She finally knew what was really going on.

Santa Claus hadn't stolen Christmas. *Candy Claws* had. The difference was small but important. *Claus* vs. *Claws.*

"What have you done with Santa?" Abigail demanded.

"Tell us where he is," ordered Andrew.

Zoë's accusation was correct. Candy Claws had taken Santa hostage. Taken him prisoner. Christmas wouldn't be in such trouble otherwise.

Candy Claws held his huge belly and laughed. "Ha, ha, ha!" Almost like Santa but not quite. He wasn't jolly.

"Get 'em, boys," he said.

On his order, dozens of candy bandits charged into view. They came from every direction, raised candy cane rifles, and took aim.

Only some fast thinking by Andrew broke up their attack.

"Here comes my eight-ten split," he shouted. "It's got lots of roll and one big hit!"

Legs spread, he skated straight into the approaching candy bandits. They fired their candy canes, but Andrew sped in too low. He easily dodged them.

CRASH! He bowled over eight, or maybe ten, of the candy bandits.

One bandit split so far that it flew toward Zoë. She snatched it out of midair like an outfielder on the run. Who knew, maybe Abigail's skills were catching? Get it, catching? Like both a cold and a baseball player.

Not even Zoë laughed at that one.

"Hook!" she exclaimed, turning the candy bandit in her hands. Then she swept it at the nearest row of bandits and yanked them offstage. Hooked crooks! In other words, she gave them the hook.

Abigail worked quickly to finish off the remaining bandits. A quick dip into her duffel bag would wrap them up. Tada, out came a volleyball net!

"Ole!" she cried and snapped the net like a bullfighter's cape. But instead of whisking it out of the way of the charging bandits, she snared them like fish in a net.

What teamwork! The heroes could be proud. Only Candy Claws wasn't impressed by their effort.

"Ha, ha, ha!" he cackled. "Sweet work. You escaped a sticky situation."

"You won't be able to say the same," Abigail scowled.

"That's right, Claws," Andrew said. "You're finished."

"History," added Zoë.

Candy Claws shook his head. "Want to know the best thing about candy? Too much will always give you a stomachache. Attack!"

Too much indeed. Because suddenly a new battalion of candy bandits rose up behind Candy Claws. There were too many to count. The heroes could only run for their lives.

CHAPTER 14:
GIFT GYSER

"This way!" Andrew shouted. "Climb the presents. Hurry!"

He and his sisters had fought well. They had defeated a nasty batch of bandits. But the army behind Candy Claws was too big. *Too much*, as Claws had said. They could not stand against it.

So they didn't stand. They ran. Right to the nearest pile of presents. Then up they climbed, using their superpowers, in a race to the top.

"Ha, ha, ha!" laughed Candy Claws. "We've got you surrounded like cookies in milk. Surrender!"

"Never!" said Abigail, but inside she wasn't so sure. She glanced at Andrew, hoping he had a plan.

He did.

"Gift gyser!" he shouted, and started to spin. Round and round he went like a human wheel. Then down and down he spun like a drill.

He went down so far that he disappeared. Around him the giant pile of presents started to tremble. Then it shook. Then it finally exploded.

BOOM!

Gifts went flying. Ribbons and bows cut through the air like streamers. Bits of paper fluttered and fell like confetti.

"It's a parade!" Abigail cheered as she tumbled safely to the floor like a gymnast.

"Hooray!" Zoë hooted.

They were safe from the explosion, like surfers riding a towering wave. It burst away from them, not at them.

The bandits weren't so fortunate. The explosion burst in their frosted faces. Down goes candy!

Presents struck from every angle. *Bonk!* A new bicycle. *Biff!* A board game. *Smack!* A new squirt gun with very good aim. Candy bandits went flying farther than the presents.

"Quit watching and run!" Andrew bellowed. He, too, had reached the ground and stopped spinning.

The same couldn't be said for the candy bandits. Most were wondering what had hit them. Their heads spun dizzily.

"Follow me!" Abigail called.

The heroes sprinted out of the building and down an alley. They turned right, took two lefts, and finally stopped to catch their breath. Little did they know that their breath wasn't all that would be caught.

A strong hand gripped Abigail and Andrew on their shoulders.

"Who are you?" someone asked from behind them.

CHAPTER 15:
LOLLYPOP LOCKUP

Andrew and Abigail gasped. They were caught! After they had run so far to escape.

They whirled, arms raised for protection. They expected to see Candy Claws or another unit of his candy corps.

What they saw was an elf. A *real* elf. Not a candy cane wannabe.

"Who are you?" the elf repeated. "I'm Ernie Elf, and these are my brothers and sisters. Meet Elsie, Ella, Edna, Eddie, and Elvis. We work for Santa. At least we used to."

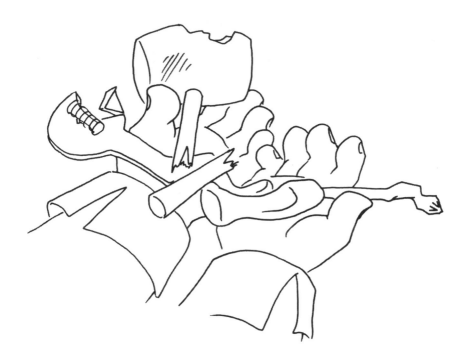

"So who do you work for now?" Andrew asked in accusation.

"I'll bet it's Candy Claws," Abigail snapped.

"Toys and toolboxes!" Ernie Elf frowned. "You've got it all wrong. We won't work for Candy Claws. We're his prisoners. See? Look."

He pushed his hands forward. On his open palms lay several broken tools. A mangled mallet, wrecked wrench, and squished screwdriver.

"Candy Claws destroyed our toy-making tools. We don't have any magic without them. We cannot escape or rescue Santa!"

The heroes blinked. "Santa is here? In Sugarglobe City?" Abigail asked. "We've got to find him."

Zoë placed a hand on her heart. "Honest," she told the elves.

Ernie and his family smiled. They believed her.

"Santa is in jail," Ernie said seriously. "He's being held in the Lollypop Lockup." The elf swallowed. "Come with me. I will show you."

Although Ernie Elf had short legs, he could run fast. He led the heroes through Sugarglobe City on a whirlwind tour. Streets streaked past, buildings blurred, and they took the turns at top speeds. The heroes were out of breath and completely lost by the time they reached the Lollypop Lockup.

"Santa is inside," Ernie Elf whispered. "Now I have to go back to my family before Candy Claws notices I'm missing. Toys and toolboxes! Good luck!"

The Lollypop Lockup was like a gingerbread house with bars in the windows. The front door, however, was wide open. Candy Claws wanted everyone to know who was being held prisoner inside.

Santa Claus! The heroes spotted him from the street, and they quickly rushed in to see him.

"Santa! Santa!" the twins cried. Never had they expected to see Santa behind bars.

And what bars they were! Like so many things in Sugarglobe City, the bars were made of candy canes.

"Ho-ho-hello, Abigail," Santa smiled. "Aloha, Andrew. Bonjour, Baby Zoë." Even in jail, he was jolly. He also remembered their names.

"Hat?" Zoë asked, noticing something odd right away. Santa wasn't wearing his trademark head-gear.

The merry old elf shrugged but continued to smile.

"Candy Claws took my ho-ho-hat," he explained. "I cannot change size without it, so I'm stuck." He tapped a bar in front of him. "I tried licking my way out, but I prefer cookies and milk."

Zoë took that as a hint. She was here to res-cue Santa, and she was always a good eater.

Chomp!

Using her super strength and her even-more-super appetite, she bit the bars in the Lollypop Lockup like a shark chewing a diver's cage. Five mouthfuls and Santa was free.

Temporarily.

"Going somewhere?" Candy Claws snarled. He had found them again. "Don't you know that it's impolite to leave before dessert?"

CHAPTER 16:
WHEN CLAWS ATTACKS

"Candy Claws!" Andrew growled. "We're putting you on the Naughty List."

At his side, Abigail nodded. "Permanently."

Of the heroes, only Zoë didn't speak. She attacked. Candy Claws had stolen Christmas and locked Santa in jail. She still had the candy cane in her mouth to prove it.

Leading with her fists, Zoë plowed into Candy Claws' enormous belly. She hit hard, but his belly hit harder: *B-O-I-N-G!*

The belly bounced back, bopping Zoë across the jail, through the wall, and into the sugary city beyond.

"Ha, ha, ha!" Candy Claws rumbled, mocking Santa's laugh and Zoë's attack. "Is that all you've got? Don't sugarcoat it. Really let me have it."

Abigail stomped the floor like an angry bull and charged. She was thinking linebacker chasing down the quarterback.

"You stole sacks of toys from so many families!" she roared. "Now I'm going to sack you!"

Candy Claws stopped her with his beard and a flick of the wrist. Yes, his beard. It was made of extra-gooey cotton candy. Quite tasty, actually, but also dangerous.

He snatched a handful with his pudgy fingers and tossed the clump at Abigail. *Splat!* Direct hit to the face. Abigail stumbled and fell.

Claws cheered! "Have seconds! I insist!" And he heaved another sticky shot. This time it gummed up Abigail's feet and legs.

Abigail was down, but not all the way out. At least she had distracted Candy Claws. Her charge gave Andrew time to attack unchallenged.

"It's the Kid's turn to roll!" he said, squealing his wheels. "Turn, roll—get it?" Then—*zoom!*—he blazed toward Candy Claws like a race car down the homestretch.

He almost made it, too. He almost reached Candy Claws. But this villain had a trick up his sleeve. Up most of his shirt, really. He could roll almost as well as Andrew.

On his belly.

Candy Claws glanced up at the last second. His eyes widened like Christmas ornaments. Then he threw himself to the floor and rolled out of the way.

Andrew whooshed past, hands grasping at Claws. He connected briefly and knocked the hat from his belt. After that, nothing.

He had mostly missed, but Claws completely connected. Lying on his stomach, he jabbed his cane through the spokes of Andrew's wheel. The result was instantaneous.

Stop. Whoa! Andrew went flying head over heels.

Claws, however, was up a second later, straddling his candy cane staff like a witch's broom. Then he and the staff floated up off the floor.

"Prepare to be caned!" he bellowed. "Candy caned!"

The tip of his staff glowed a sinister red.

CHAPTER 17:
AQUA-BABY

Abigail tore the sticky cotton candy off her feet, rolled onto her hands and knees, and looked ready to charge. Only a warning from Andrew stopped her.

"Stay down!" he hissed.

Ahead of them, Candy Claws was already charging. Charging his weapon, that is. The tip of his candy cane staff blazed red and shot forth a beam of sparkling energy.

Z-z-z-zap!

Candy Claws' aim was perfect. His shot
streaked straight at the twins. It would have struck
them, too, if not for a giant obstacle.

"Ho-ho-here I come!" Santa boomed cheer-
fully. His hat was back on his head where it be-
longed, and he looked like himself again. Like himself except three times bigger than normal.

You see, Santa wasn't just wearing his hat. He
was using its special Christmas magic to change size.
He could use it to shrink down to fit into any chimney. Most everyone knew that. But he could also
use it to grow big enough to pick up the heaviest
present. That's what he was doing now.

Santa was massive, gigantic, and huge! He was so big, in fact, that he made a perfect target. Not even a blindfolded Cyclops could miss him.

"Ho-ho-hey!" the oversized elf exclaimed.

Candy Claws' cane ray connected in a belly bullseye. *Z-z-z-zap!* Santa didn't stand a chance. The rotten ray turned him into a snowman, just like the heroes' parents and all their friends back in Traverse City.

"No!" the twins wailed. Not Santa, and not again! First they had lost Zoë. Now Santa had been caned. If they didn't move, they would be next.

So Abigail sprinted and Andrew rolled, right around Candy Claws and out the door. The pair would have pushed on, too, had they not nearly tripped over their baby sister.

"Howdy!" Zoë waved at them cheerily.

To her siblings' surprise, Zoë was floating in a hole in the ground. She looked like an ice fisherman who had decided to take a swim.

Zoë giggled and splashed in the water. "Hole," she said.

"Sure is," Andrew said impatiently. "You're in a hole. Now let's get you—"

Abigail cut him off. "Andrew, look. The hole is growing!"

Andrew did a double take. The hole was growing. The sugar around it was melting like ice on a warm spring day.

Andrew could have smacked himself. He should have thought of it sooner. Sugar dissolved in water. It melted. That was why Candy Claws had built a globe around his city. He couldn't allow it to get wet. Water would melt Sugarglobe City like a wicked witch.

"Zoë, can you give this city a bath?" Andrew asked rapidly. He had a plan, but there wasn't time to explain. He hoped Zoë caught on.

She did. She nodded and took a deep breath. Then down into the icy waters Zoë dove like Aquaman getting ready to call for help. She was Aqua-baby! One bath coming right up.

First she sent her thoughts out to a nearby shark. "Hammerhead!"

Then to a whale. "Humpback!"

And finally to something more unusual. "Horns!"

She thought those three creatures were best, and knew it was up to them to respond. All she could do after that was hope. The heroes were running out of time.

CHAPTER 18:
CHRISTMAS MIRACLE

The twins stared anxiously at the hole where Zoë had disappeared. How long would it be until she returned? Seconds, minutes, hours? Candy Claws would find them soon. Hurry, Zoë, please!

Z-z-z-zap!

Just like that, soon became now. Candy Claws arrived, and he wasn't wasting time. He was shooting first and asking questions later. If asking questions meant more shooting.

The twins narrowly escaped by splitting up. Abigail ran right, and Andrew looped left. Candy Claws bombarded the empty space between them with shots.

Boom! Boom! Boom!

The ground erupted where the lasers landed. Candy Claws meant business this time, as in putting the competition out of business. His candy cane wasn't set on snowman anymore. It was set on *no man*. No one. No more.

Boom! Boom!

BOOM!

The sixth explosion heaved the heroes into the air. In fact, all of Sugarglobe City rumbled as if caught in an earthquake. Even Candy Claws toppled over.

"That last blast was a doozey!" Andrew gasped, whirling through the air like a wobbly wheel.

"A doozey? You're dizzy!" Abigail shouted. "That blast was Zoë. She's the bomb. You better hold your breath!"

Sploosh!

Andrew felt what was happening before he saw it. No sooner had Abigail shouted than a tidal wave crashed over his head.

A tidal wave? Water! That could mean only one thing. Zoë was back, and she had brought friends. *Big* friends by the sound of it.

S-P-L-O-O-S-H! Big friends by the *feel* of it, too.

"Hydro!" the littlest hero cheered.   She was back, all right, and with enough water for everyone.

Zoë was sitting on the back of a hammerhead shark. The pair had burst up through the ground and were squirting water from their mouths. The scene reminded Zoë of the time she had battled Dinozilla, a gigantic dinosaur made of bones.*

*See Heroes A2Z #4: Digging For Dinos

Sploosh! Behind her and the shark came a narwhal, slashing through the ground with its sharp horn. *Sploosh!* Followed by an enormous humpback whale. Both were squirting water like trained firefighters.

Under the oceanic onslaught, Sugarglobe City didn't stand a chance. Every splash of water, every dribble and drop, melted the city a little bit more. In minutes, its tasty buildings looked like drippy candles. The sweet, sugary city had gone soggy and sour.

Even Santa melted, from snowman back to ho-ho-ho man. His red suit wasn't even damp. Give it up for Christmas magic.

"I'll take that," he said to Candy Claws. Then before the villain could react, Santa snatched Claws' candy cane and snapped it over his knee. "You'll be getting coal in your stocking this year, Candy Claws."

Simple but effective. Santa was back in charge. Sugarglobe City was no more, and Candy Claws had been stripped of his power. Even all of the people who had been turned into snowmen melted back to normal.

Christmas was almost saved. Almost but not yet. There were still presents to be delivered, and morning was coming soon. How would Santa ever finish in time?

He thought for a moment and then smiled at Zoë. His eyes sparkled playfully. "Zoë, with your gift of flight, won't you guide my sleigh tonight?"

Andrew's eyes bugged, and Abigail's jaw dropped. Santa had just asked their baby sister to ride up front with Rudolph. Talk about a Christmas miracle!

Zoë blushed and stared at her feet. "Honored," she answered softly. That meant yes.

So while Zoë and the reindeer pulled, Abigail and Andrew joined Santa in his sleigh. It was a wild, windy ride none of them would forget. At sunrise, they were exhausted but done. They had delivered every present. Santa thanked the heroes for their courage and told them to be careful. Like Candy Claws, a villain could pretend to be anyone, even the coach of a little league baseball team in …

Book #9:
Ivy League All-Stars

Fighting Crime Before Bedtime

... and more!

Visit
www.realheroesread.com
for the latest news

Visit the Website

realheroesread.com

Watch Heroes A2Z Mini-Movies
Meet Authors Charlie & David
Read Sample Chapters
See Fan Artwork
Join the Free Fan Club
Invite Charlie & David to Your School
Lots More!

Also by David Anthony and Charles David

Monsters. Magic. Mystery.

Visit
www.realheroesread.com
to learn more

#1: Cauldron Cooker's Night

#2: Skull in the Birdcage

#3: Early Winter's Orb

#4: Voyage to Silvermight
The Dragonsbane Horn Book One

#5: Trek Through Tanglewood
The Dragonsbane Horn Book Two

#6: Hunt the Hollow Deep
The Dragonsbane Horn Book Three

#7: The Ninespire Experiment

#8: Aware of the Wolf

Want to Order Your Very Own Autographed Heroes A2Z or Knightscares Book?

Here's How:

(1) Check the books you want on the next page.
(2) Fill out the address information at the bottom.
(3) Add up the total price for the books you want.

Heroes A2Z cost $4.99 each.
Knightscares cost $5.99 each.

(4) Add $1.50 shipping & handling per book.
(5) Michigan residents include 6% sales tax.
(6) Make check or money order out to
Sigil Publishing, LLC
(7) Mail payment and the next page to:

Real Heroes Read!
P.O. Box 654
Union Lake, MI 48387

Thank You!

Please allow 3-4 weeks for shipping

☐ Heroes A2Z #1: Alien Ice Cream

☐ Heroes A2Z #2: Bowling Over Halloween

☐ Heroes A2Z #3: Cherry Bomb Squad

☐ Heroes A2Z #4: Digging For Dinos

☐ Heroes A2Z #5: Easter Egg Haunt

☐ Heroes A2Z #6: Fowl Mouthwash

☐ Heroes A2Z #7: Guitar Rocket Star

☐ Heroes A2Z #8: Holiday Holdup

☐ Knightscares #1: Cauldron Cooker's Night

☐ Knightscares #2: Skull in the Birdcage

☐ Knightscares #3: Early Winter's Orb

☐ Knightscares #4: Voyage to Silvermight

☐ Knightscares #5: Trek Through Tangleroot

☐ Knightscares #6: Hunt for Hollowdeep

☐ Knightscares #7: The Ninespire Experiment

☐ Knightscares #8: Aware of the Wolf

Total $ Enclosed: _____

Autograph To: _____

Name: _____

Address: _____

City, State, Zip: _____

ABIGAIL

TRIPLE A
ALL AMERICAN ATHLETE

ANDREW

KID ROLL

ZOË

ZUPER ZOË

DRAW
YOUR OWN
SUPERHERO

We want to see your drawings. Make up a super-hero and send a drawing of it to us. Use plain white paper only. We will put your hero on our website.

Mail your drawings along with your name and address to:

Real Heroes Read!
P.O. Box 654
Union Lake, MI   48387

REAL HEROES DRAW!

realheroesread.com

Email the Authors

Charlie:
charlie@sigilpublishing.com

David:
david@sigilpublishing.com

Visit the Website

REAL
HEROES
READ!

realheroesread.com

Sigil Publishing, LLC

P.O. Box 824
Leland, MI 49654

Email:
info@sigilpublishing.com

About the Illustrator
Lys Blakeslee

Lys graduated from Grand Valley State University in Michigan where she earned a degree in Illustration.

She has always loved to read, and devoted much of her childhood to devouring piles of books from the library.

She lives in Wyoming, MI with her wonderful parents, two goofy cats, and one extra-loud parakeet.

Thank you, Lys!